JUV
FIC

Sandburg, Carl, 1878-
1967.

More rootabagas.

$18.00

MORE ROOTABAGAS

MORE ROOTABAGAS

Stories by
CARL SANDBURG

Pictures by
PAUL O. ZELINSKY

Collected and with a Foreword by
George Hendrick

ALFRED A. KNOPF • New York

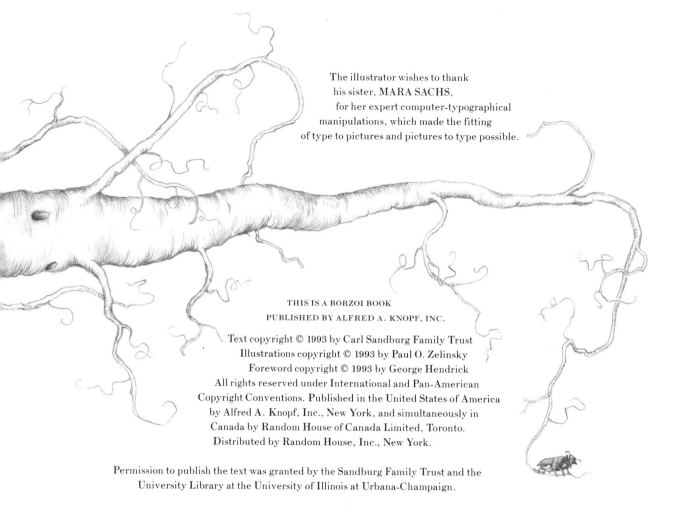

The illustrator wishes to thank
his sister, MARA SACHS,
for her expert computer-typographical
manipulations, which made the fitting
of type to pictures and pictures to type possible.

THIS IS A BORZOI BOOK
PUBLISHED BY ALFRED A. KNOPF, INC.

Text copyright © 1993 by Carl Sandburg Family Trust
Illustrations copyright © 1993 by Paul O. Zelinsky
Foreword copyright © 1993 by George Hendrick

Permission to publish the text was granted by the Sandburg Family Trust and the
University Library at the University of Illinois at Urbana-Champaign.

Library of Congress Cataloging-in-Publication Data. Sandburg, Carl, 1878–1967.
More rootabagas / by Carl Sandburg ; illustrated by Paul O. Zelinsky.
p. cm. Summary: A selection of Sandburg's fanciful, humorous short stories
peopled with such characters as the Potato Face Blind Man, Susan Slackentwist, and Dippy the Wisp.
ISBN 0-679-80070-0 (trade) ISBN 0-679-90070-5 (lib. bdg.)
1. Children's stories, American. [1. Short stories. 2. Fantasy.] I. Zelinsky, Paul O., ill.
II. Title. III. Title: More rutabagas. PZ7.S1972Mo 1993 [Fic]—dc20 93-14930

The art was prepared using colored pencils on plastivellum drafting film.
Manufactured in the United States of America 10 9 8 7 6 5 4 3 2 1

FOREWORD

WE LEARN SOMETHING of Carl Sandburg's special feelings for his children in a letter dated 1920: "The kids at home are a tantalization of loveliness . . . They are a loan, only a loan, out of nowhere, back to nowhere, babbling, wild-flying—they die every day like flowers shedding petals—and come on again."

When the time came that his daughters—nicknamed "Spink," "Skabootch" and "Swipes"—began begging their father for bedtime stories, Sandburg searched out books that might interest them, and him. Long an admirer of traditional tales, especially those of Hans Christian Andersen, Sandburg was disappointed to find no satisfactory *American* fairy tales. "I wanted something more in the American lingo," he later complained to a biographer. So he decided to write his own stories—"tales with American fooling in them." And "kid books," he said, "are the anarchs of language and speech." Sandburg would publish three volumes of these American fairy tales: *Rootabaga Stories* (1922), *Rootabaga Pigeons* (1923) and *Potato Face* (1930).

In writing the Rootabaga stories, Sandburg had, according to the *New York Times*, "gone to the American prairies, to the Middle West towns and cities, to the great American Corn Belt, and conceived a series of tales that smack mightily of American soil. Even to the cadence of his prose, so often implicit of poetry, the reader will find an American spirit."

Sandburg continued to write Rootabaga stories, but so involved did he become in researching and writing his monumental six-volume biography of Abraham Lincoln that no others were published. Of the many dozens of these stories, I have chosen the ten I feel most reflect Sandburg's incomparable storytelling magic.

"I am not sure," Sandburg remarked late in life, "but when the rest of my work fades out there will be two or three Rootabaga stories standing."

The "Old Slicker" might have been too modest. These fairy tales are true American classics.

—GEORGE HENDRICK
Professor of English,
University of Illinois at Urbana-Champaign

CONTENTS

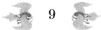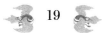

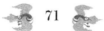

A Girl Named Silver Pitchers
Tells a Story About Egypt,
Jesse James and Spanish Onions

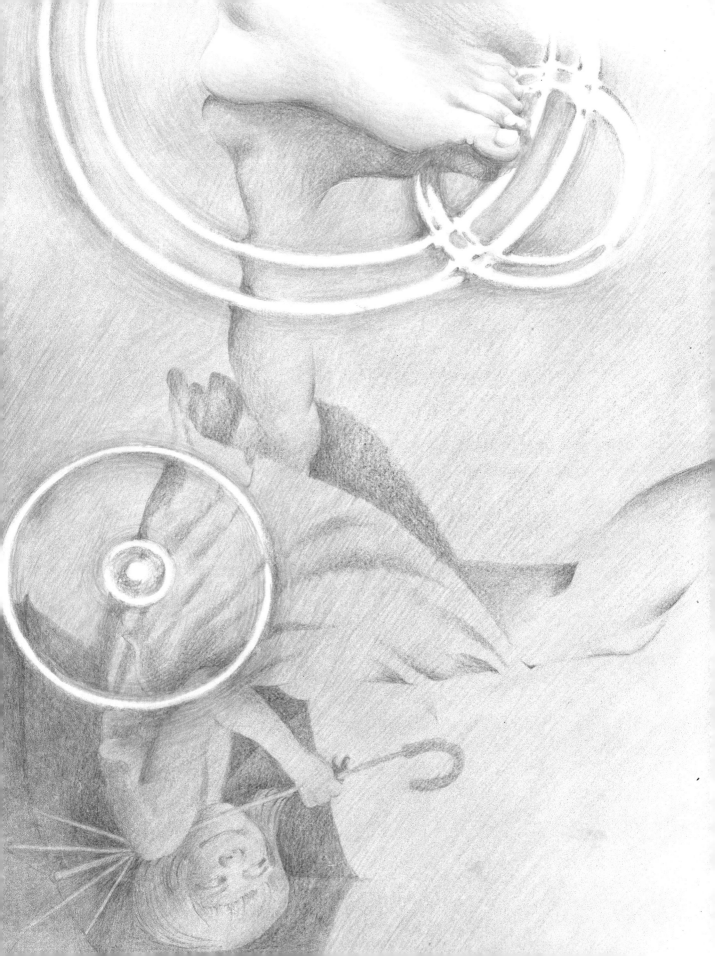

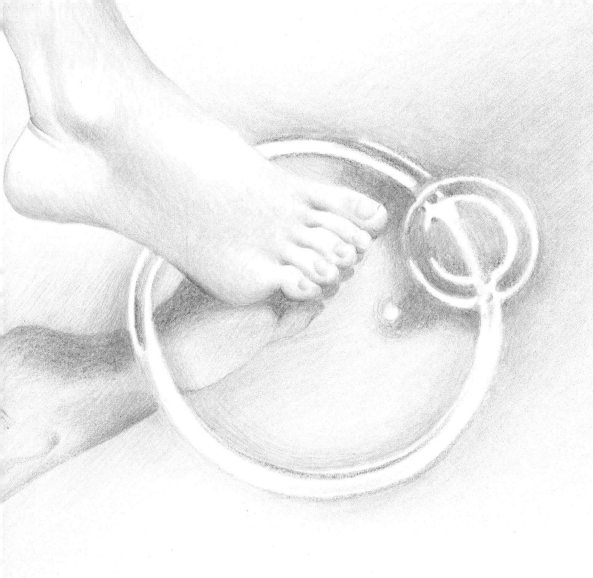

ONE EVENING IN
ROOTABAGA COUNTRY,
WHEN THE MOON WAS SHINING AND
making gold pools where the raindrops spread their circles
on the pavement, the girl named Silver Pitchers came to the
Potato Face Blind Man and they had a long talk.

"It is a misty moisty evening and everything is mystical in the moonshine," she said to him the first time she spoke.

"Yes, it is so mystical and the moonshine makes so many gold pools where the raindrops spread their circles, it is lonesome and I would rather hear a story than tell one," answered the Potato Face.

Then Silver Pitchers began telling the old man about her three rabbits named Egypt, Jesse James and Spanish Onions.

"Egypt is the black lonesome one," she began, "and on her white nose Egypt has three black stripes. But on her white tail she has five black triangles. And around her white neck are seven black rings all wrapped around in circles."

"If I ever meet Egypt I will know her and I will say, 'Hello, Egypt, you little black and white rascal,' " said Potato Face.

"Jesse James is all covered with finger marks and thumb prints. He is white as snow all over. He was born white as snow. But he is soft on his skin and soft in his hair, and whenever anybody lifts him up, looks in his eyes and puts him down, the marks of the finger marks and the prints of the thumb prints are all over Jesse."

"And I guess I will know Jesse if I ever meet him and I will pick him up and say, 'Hello, Jesse James,' " murmured the old man.

"Spanish Onions is a rabbit with a flat behind from sitting so much. He has a long flat tail he sits on. Whenever he sits down he makes a circle with his tail and then sits down inside the circle."

"Maybe I will know Spanish Onions by his long flat tail and maybe not," broke in the Potato Face, "but if I do I will pick him up by the ears and tell him, 'Hello, Spanish Onions, you are the rabbit Silver Pitchers tells about.' "

"All the year I keep Egypt, Jesse James and Spanish Onions, all three rabbits, hutched in their hutches," went on Silver Pitchers.

"That is the way to keep rabbits— hutch them in their hutches," murmured the old man.

"On the first of November," she said, "they jump out of the hutches where they are hutched. They run away and come back with stories. And they are so proud and so particular about their stories that I can't ask them any questions.

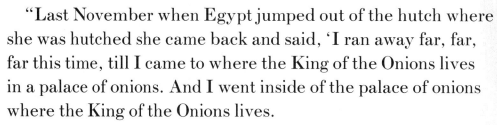

"Last November when Egypt jumped out of the hutch where she was hutched she came back and said, 'I ran away far, far, far this time, till I came to where the King of the Onions lives in a palace of onions. And I went inside of the palace of onions where the King of the Onions lives.

" 'I expected to see onions and onions in the palace. But instead of onions the palace was full of cats. Upstairs and downstairs, all over the palace, were cats.

" 'Blue, all over blue, one ear cream, the other ear orange, were the cats. And they carried looking glasses in their shoes.

" ' "We can never remember which ear is cream and which ear is orange — we carry the looking glasses in our shoes to take out and look at our ears and see which ear is cream and which ear is orange," they told me.

" 'I stayed there in the palace of the King of the Onions all the time I was away. The biggest and fattest of the cats was named Fat Philadelphia Pussy. The littlest and the skinniest of all the cats was named Hoboken Kitty-kitty. I shall remember a long time the teeny weeny looking glass that Hoboken Kitty-kitty carried in her foot to see

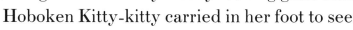

which ear is cream and which ear orange. I said good-by to all the cats, good-by to the King of the Onions. And they all said to me, "Good-by, Egypt, come back next year, Egypt." And that's all.'

"Of course, when Egypt says that's all,

that's all. You can ask any questions you want to and Egypt only
sticks out her tongue and cleans the stripes on her nose,
the five triangles on her tail and the seven black rings around
her white neck."

"What happened to Jesse James?" asked the Potato Face
Blind Man.

"Jesse James came running back and he said, 'I ran away, far,
far, far away, till I came to where the King of the Paper Sacks
lives in a palace of paper sacks. And I went inside of the palace
where the King of the Paper Sacks lives.

" 'I expected to see paper sacks everywhere. But instead of
paper sacks everywhere the palace was full of pink and purple
peanuts walking up and down the stairs washing their faces.

" 'In the evening after the sunset all the pink and purple
peanuts made paper sacks. First they made the paper, then they
made the sacks. They they stacked the sacks into high stacks of
sacks.

" 'And the King of the Paper Sacks walked around among
them, watching them and saying, "If anybody asks you who
I am, you tell them I am the King of the Paper Sacks."

" 'There was one little pink peanut with pink toes answered
one time, "Say it again—who do you think you are?" And
it made the king bitter in his feelings. He reached out his
hand and took a hundred pink peanuts with pink toes
and threw them into a big paper sack.

" 'When I went away, he shook me by the hand and said, "Good-by, Jesse James. If anybody asks you, please tell them you saw the King of the Paper Sacks."

" 'And the palace doors, windows and roof were filled with pink and purple peanuts standing on their legs calling, "Good-by, Jesse James, come back again next year, good-by, Jesse James." And that's all.' "

"What happened to Spanish Onions?" asked the Potato Face Blind Man.

"He came running back and he said, 'I ran away, far, far, far away, till I came to where the King of the Buttons lives in a palace of buttons. And I went inside of the palace where the King of the Buttons lives.

" 'I expected to see buttons all over the palace. But instead of buttons the palace was full of scissors.

" 'Upstairs and downstairs, all over the palace, there were scissors. Sometimes they were tired and they sat down on the stairs and went to sleep or they stood up in the corners and went to sleep or they hung themselves on the chandeliers and went to sleep.

" 'But most of the time they were snipping, walking up and down the stairs snipping and snipping like scissors always do.

" 'At half past six in the morning and half past six in the evening the King of the Buttons walked back and forth among the scissors and asked them, "Why am I the King of the Buttons?" And they always answered, "Because we are the scissors in the palace of the King of the Buttons."

" 'The last night I was there they gave me a big dinner. First was clam pie. And they cut the clam pie with scissors. Then came chicken pie. And they cut the chicken pie with scissors.

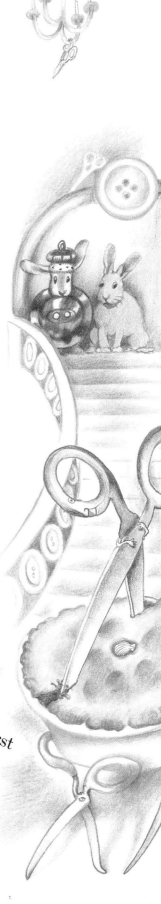

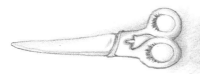

" 'Last of all was peach pie and they opened the peach pie and cut it straight and even with scissors.

" 'The morning I went away the doors, windows and roof of the palace of the King of the Buttons were filled with scissors snipping good-by to me and telling me, "Come back next year, Spanish Onions." And that's all.' "

"Do you know," said the Potato Face Blind Man, "I am sure if I ever meet Egypt or Jesse James or Spanish Onions, I will know them soon as I see them. And when you feed them tomorrow morning in the hutches where they are hutched, will you tell them their stories kept me from being lonesome tonight, even when the moonshine coming down on the rainpools couldn't keep me from being lonesome."

"I will tell them," said Silver Pitchers.

"And if you ever get a chance, please ask Jesse James to ask the King of the Paper Sacks next year where all the paper sacks go when they are gone."

"I will," said Silver Pitchers, "and I'll ask Spanish Onions to find out which is easier, for a scissors to sleep sitting down on a stairway or standing up in a corner or hanging on a chandelier. And I'll ask Egypt to find out why the King of the Onions has his palace full of blue cats with looking glasses to see which ear is cream and which ear orange."

So they said good-night to each other and went home across the rainpools shining with the moongold.

The Story of
Peter Potato Blossom Wishes
and How She Went Down into
Rootabaga Country and Came Back
with Five Sky Blue Whispering Cats

IF YOU TAKE ONE
OF THE WHISPERING
SKY BLUE CATS AND HOLD IT UP
against the sky when the sky is clear and blue, you can
hardly see the cat because it is sky blue.

And if you listen to the whispering sky blue cat with one ear and listen to a whispering wind when the wind whispers soft, you can hardly tell which is which, because the whisper of the whispering sky blue cat is so much like the whisper of a whispering wind.

So this story is about the secrets whispered by the sky blue cats to the men and women of the Village of Cream Puffs and the how and the wherefore of how they whispered the secrets.

The prettiest girl in the Village of Cream Puffs was Peter Potato Blossom Wishes. Her father was Mister Wishes and her mother was Missus Wishes. When she was asked why her name was Peter Potato Blossom Wishes, she always answered, "Because my father, Mr. Wishes, wishes it, and because my mother, Mrs. Wishes, wishes it."

And it was this girl, Peter Potato Blossom Wishes, who first brought to the Village of Cream Puffs the whispering cats whose blue hair is blue as the sky, and whose whispering secrets sound like the secrets of the whispering wind.

One summer long long ago, when all these things happened, Peter Potato Blossom Wishes went away from the Village of Cream Puffs down into the Rootabaga Country to visit relations. While she was in the Rootabaga Country she saw many wonderful things. She learned the Rootabaga language and how the Rootabaga people talk, not only with their tongues but with their thumbs. (Some of their words they don't know how to say except with their thumbs; it would surprise you to learn how many things you can say with your thumbs when you are speaking to people who understand your language.) And she learned the Rootabaga dance which is danced by the Rootabagas in the fields at night when the harvest moon time comes.

And when Peter Potato Blossom Wishes came back from her trip to the Rootabaga Country, the people of the Village of Cream Puffs asked her, "Where have you been?"

She answered, "Down in Rootabaga Country."

"What did you do down in the Rootabaga Country?"

"Visited."

"Visited who?"

"Visited my relations, first my poor relations, then my rich relations, then my relations who are neither poor nor rich but halfway between poor and rich relations."

"What did your poor relations give you to bring back to remember them by?"

"They gave me their love and their blessings."

"And what did the halfway relations, neither poor nor rich, give you to bring back to remember them by?"

"They gave me their love and their blessings and a basket of rutabagas."

"And what did your rich relations give you to bring back to remember them by?"

"They gave me their love and their blessings and a basket of rutabagas... and five whispering sky blue cats."

And that was how the whispering sky blue cats with the mystery of the sky in their hair and the mystery of the wind in their soft voices came with their secrets to the Village of Cream Puffs.

And now as Peter Potato Blossom Wishes grew up there were women came to her and asked if they could hear the whispering cats whisper their secrets.

"There are only two kinds of women they whisper to," said Peter. "The sky blue cats whisper to women who know they are beautiful and to women who wonder whether they are beautiful."

And one by one the women who knew they were beautiful took the special cat that whispered only for the women who knew they were beautiful. For each one the cat sat on her shoulder and whispered into her ear, "You are today beautiful as a poem of the open sky and the morning sunrise in early summer on the bashful fields, p-e-r-h-a-p-s, and tomorrow you shall be more beautiful, p-e-r-h-a-p-s."

And to each of the women who wondered whether she was beautiful, the whispering sky blue cat whispered, "You are today beautiful as a poem of the open sky and the morning sunrise in early summer on the bashful fields, p-e-r-h-a-p-s, and tomorrow you shall be more beautiful, p-e-r-h-a-p-s."

Also while Peter Potato Blossom Wishes was growing up there were men came to her and asked if they could hear the whispering cats whisper their secrets.

"There are only two kinds of men they whisper to," said Peter. "The sky blue cats whisper to men who know they are strong and to men who wonder whether they are strong."

One by one the men who knew they were strong took the special cat that whispered only for the men who knew they were strong. For each one the cat sat on his shoulder and whispered into his ear, "You are today strong as the rock that holds the great bowl of the sea and keeps it from spilling onto the moon, p-e-r-h-a-p-s, and tomorrow you shall be stronger yet, p-e-r-h-a-p-s."

To each man who wondered whether he was strong, the whispering blue cat for that man whispered, "You are today

25

as strong as the rock that holds the great bowl of the sea and keeps it from spilling onto the moon, p-e-r-h-a-p-s, and tomorrow you shall be stronger yet, p-e-r-h-a-p-s.''

And there were still other women who did not know whether they were beautiful and never wondered about it. And there were men who did not know whether they were strong and never wondered about it. For each one of these Peter Potato Blossom Wishes placed the fifth sky blue cat on the shoulder where the cat could whisper soft like a soft wind into the ear of the woman or the man. For each one of them the cat whispered, ''Wishes are for the wisher; by and by, maybe everything you wish for will come true; wish your wishes deep into your heart and after a time your wishes will be written on your face and the wishing winds who hunt for all wishers will know your wishes and will go hunting for you; by and by, all wishes come true, by and by, by and by.''

There were men who said, ''We hear what they say but we do not understand their meaning.'' So too there were women who said, ''We hear what they whisper but we do not understand their meaning.''

And Peter Potato Blossom Wishes, who was the prettiest girl in the Village of Cream Puffs, answered them, ''What they say is what they learned from the whispering winds, and the meaning is the same as the meaning of the whispering wind. Just as the blue of their sky blue hair has only the meaning of sky blue when the sky is clear and blue, so their whispering has only the meaning of the whispering wind.''

How the Caterpillar Told Secrets
to a Spink Bug and a Huck

A SPINK BUG AND

A HUCK WHO LEARNED

HOW TO BE GOOD PALS WERE TAKING

a trip to the famous moon baths in the hill country halfway
north of the Village of Liver-and-Onions and the Village of
Cream Puffs.

They met a seven-ring caterpillar.

"Where you going?" they said.

"You mean what place I'm going?"

"Ex-   actly."

"Cater-   pillars don't go no place,   I thought you
knowed   that much, you being   a spink bug,"
and he waved his head in the air and   waved a long
wavy salute to the spink bug, "and   you   being a
huck bug," and he waved his head   in the air
and waved a long wavy salute to the huck bug.

"Caterpillars can be nice when they want to, can't they?"
whispered the spink bug to the huck. But to the caterpillar,
speaking out loud, the spink said, "Why do you do this if you
ain't got no place to go to? You keep a-moving and a-moving
and you look like you wanted to get from one place to go to
another place. That was why we asked you where you
was going."

"I'm listening, go on," said the caterpillar.

"Don't you feel yourself going somewhere? Don't you know
if you keep on going like you're going, in a million years you'll
be a thousand miles from here?"

"I know all about it. I   stand by what I said to
you first. I ain't going   no place at all.
I'm just a-mooching   along. Being a
caterpillar, I was   born to mooch.
If I didn't mooch like this   I couldn't live with
the caterpillars and be one.
All caterpillars mooch."

"This is a very intelligent
caterpillar," said the huck bug
out of the side of his mouth,

30

whispering
to the spink. "Yes,
he's onto himself—ask
him more," said the spink out of
the side of his mouth, whispering it
with syllables.

"Most respectfully we ask you to tell us more about
mooching," spoke the spink out loud to the caterpillar.

"Mooching is how caterpillars measure," was the answer from
the seven-ring caterpillar. "There would never be no inches if it
wasn't for the caterpillar mooching. Two inches came from two
caterpillar mooches. Look—" and the caterpillar mooched two
mooches. "And six inches came from six caterpillar mooches."
And the caterpillar mooched six mooches. "The first inch ever
was a mooch inch," he said as he mooched one mooch to show
how much. "All the millions of miles and mileses in the world is
inches and every inch is just a mooch. Wherever you go it's just
so many mooches. Caterpillars don't care where they are going
or what places there are to go to. It's *how far,* how many inches
and every inch a mooch, that's all caterpillars ask about. And
now having answered your questions respectfully may I ask
you a question for you to answer respectfully, Mr. Spink?"

"Most respectfully you may ask any question and most
distinguished I shall answer if it is in my possibilities to be so
distinguished," replied the spink.

"Why do you have a big hump like a gunnysack on your
back on purpose all the time?" came from the caterpillar.

"I give you a distinguished answer as I promised
respectfully," the spink bug spinked. "The hump is half
and half. Half is what I did yesterday. Half is what

31

I am going to do tomorrow. It looks just like that, don't you
think so?"

"Indeed, I believe you are quite correct, quite so, quite so,
and so I must mooch along."

"Before you mooch along tell us respectfully why you have
seven black rings all around your brown hair coat. Did they

forget any rings or was seven the right number?"

"Long ago, long before the week was invented with its seven days from beginning to end, there were no black rings on the fuzz-brown coat of the caterpillar. Then the week was invented, with seven days for every week. And at the same time the seven black rings were invented for caterpillars to remember how many week days."

"Do caterpillars forget easy?" the huck bug hucked.

"On forgetful days all caterpillars have it hard to remember. But on the good remember days they never, never forget."

"What do you forget on your forgetful days?"

"Seven things we forget. We forget to eat breakfast. We forget to eat dinner. We forget to eat supper. We forget to go to bed. We forget what our mothers said. We forget what our fathers said. We forget to come in out of the rain if we have no umbrella."

"Is it not terrible to forget seven things like those on your forgetful days? Are you not afraid you will die some day when you forget such seven things to be done every day?"

"No, that is the secret of being a happy caterpillar. That is why we have seven black rings. Each ring makes us remember on the forgetful days. The first ring here on the back of my neck tells me to eat breakfast. So I always have breakfast. The second ring tells me to eat dinner. So I always have dinner. So each one of the other rings tells me to eat supper, go to bed, remember what my mother said, what my father said. And last of all this black ring down near the end of my tail tells me to come in out of the rain if I have no umbrella."

"Caterpillars are distinguished intelligent," the spink bug whispered in syllables out of the side of his mouth to the huck.

"May we apologize to you for thanking us very kindly out of your gratitude?" outbursted the huck bug. "You have given us new syllables and new adjectives and we thank you a thousand times for learning us how to learn more knowledge to be useful."

"And I wish to thank you for syllables and adjectives," said the caterpillar. "Most of all I thank you, Mr. Spink, for telling me your hump on your back is half and half, half what you did yesterday and half what you're going to do tomorrow. I shall tell it to my mother caterpillar who has seven rings and to my father caterpillar who has seven rings and to my brother and sister caterpillars who each have seven black rings on their fuzz-brown coats."

And they said good-by and the spink bug and the huck, who were perfectly good pals and understood each other without any fancy language, went on with their trip to the famous moon baths in the hill country halfway north of the Village of Liver-and-Onions and the Village of Cream Puffs.

How Susan Slackentwist Sang a Song
to a Cornfield Scarecrow

THE SUMMER
AFTER THE WINTER

WHEN HENRY HAGGLYHOAGLY PLAYED
the guitar with his mittens on one cold winter night under
the window of Susan Slackentwist, the daughter of the

rutabaga king, there came to these sweethearts a bump of hard luck. Sometimes, you know, hard luck comes straight along like a big wagon in the middle of the road and you see it's coming and you know what to expect. Then sometimes hard luck drops down all of a sudden like a pail of slickery slickish sticky whitewash tumbling down out of a tree on top of your head. That was the way hard luck bumped Henry Hagglyhoagly and Susan Slackentwist.

"I seen enough of that Henry Hagglyhoagly around this place and I don't want to see no more of him around here," said Old Man Slackentwist to his daughter Susan one Saturday night when there was a green moon shaped like a coal bucket coming up just beyond the humps of the rutabaga plants that lay for miles and miles west of the rutabaga king's house.

"Father, Father, why are you so cruel? He ain't done no wrong to nobody," said Susan Slackentwist, putting a long coil of her corn-colored hair around and over her left ear.

"I'm done having that rascal of a rapscallion around this place; every time he comes around he talks about string beans, string beans, always saying string beans looks more beautiful than rutabagas. I won't have anybody come to my house and see my daughter, saying string beans looks more beautiful than rutabagas looks beautiful."

"Father, Father, you are too cruel, he never said it like you say he said it," said Susan Slackentwist, this time putting a long coil of her corn-colored hair

around and over her *right* ear.

"If he never said it like I said he
said, then how did he say it?"

"He said rutabagas looks beautiful in the
autumn weather when the white frost comes
along and pinches their ears and puts white
hats on 'em and makes 'em look like thousands and
thousands of frost rabbits singing an early song to winter.
And he said in the summertime the string beans looks
beautiful when they got their green bonnets fixed over their
heads and the green strings fastened under their green
chinny-chin-chins like as how they was hoping summer would
stay a long long time 'cause summer felt so good. That's what
he said," and this time Susan Slackentwist took both her hands
(try it yourself) and put both coils of her corn-colored hair, one
over her left ear, one over her right ear.

"Susanna, cruel or no cruel, wrong or no wrong, you take it from me, I ain't going to have that Henry Hagglyhoagly party around these here premises—him and his string beans looks more beautiful than rutabagas keeps away from hereaways."

"Father, Father, is there no justice, is there no mercy?"

"Daughter, I have spoke my spik."

Then there were shadows. The daughter took down from over her ears the long coils of corn-colored hair, wept in the shadows and sang soft to herself, "Cru-el, cru-el, there is no justice, there is no mercy."

And the father stood in the shadows with his shoulders high over the door sill, leaning and looking out into the cool summer night, muttering, "String beans more beautiful than rutabagas—I'll show him—I have spoke my spik."

The next night there came up over the horizon off the rutabaga fields a golden cheese moon. The fields were slumbering, the moon was slumbering, and the gold and the cheese in the moon must have been slumbering.

"Where are you going, Susan?" said Old Man Slackentwist to his daughter as she tied under her chin the strings of her string bean bonnet.

"Out in the fields, Father, to talk with the scarecrow," said Susan as she covered her corn-colored hair with the rim of her string bean bonnet.

And the father stood in the door while the daughter ran, ran and ran, singing gold and cheese songs to the golden cheese moon, singing in the slumbrous night, all the way out to the middle of the big rutabaga field where the scarecrow stood with his arms out

(like this)

and his head hanging (like this)

and his knees kind of sagging and crumply

(like this).

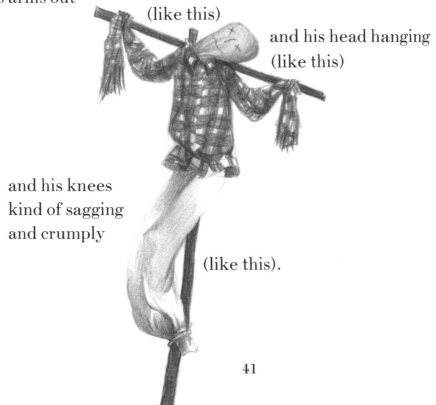

41

And her father, watching at the door, saw her sit down in
front of the scarecrow. And way off he could hear her singing
a sad-like song about the golden cheese moon, the slumbering
night and her string bean bonnet, and the beauty of the long
low miles of rutabaga fields.

Then the father heard no more singing. He stood with
his shoulders high over the door sill just a-listening, just

a-listening. He thought Susan had quit singing. But she hadn't.
She was singing a soft song, the softest kind of a sweetheart
song. B-e-c-a-u-s-e where she sat singing she could look right
straight up into the face and form of the scarecrow—and right
up against the face and form of the scarecrow was Henry
Hagglyhoagly, wriggled and twisted and crumpled, holding his
arms out with the scarecrow arms, and hanging his head and

sagging his knees just like the scarecrow. In the light of
the golden cheese moon you would have to step up
close to see it was not only a scarecrow but a scarecrow
and Henry Hagglyhoagly.

So she sang to him there with a low song and he answered
there with a low song even though it is not easy to sing with
your head hanging like a scarecrow head and your arms
hanging like scarecrow arms.

The Story of How Dippy the Wisp
and Ax Me No Questions
Learned About the Village
of Pick Ups

ONE MORNING
DIPPY THE WISP ASKED
THE POTATO FACE BLIND MAN TO TELL A
story, but he wouldn't. And the morning before, both Dippy
the Wisp and Ax Me No Questions had asked him to tell a

story, but he wouldn't. They coaxed him with their sweetest voices, "Tell us the one about the Village of Pick Ups." But he wouldn't. He laughed them away with laughing out, "I would rather and lots rather tell you about the little birds that fly upside down on Tuesdays. I would rather tell you about the big onkatonk that flies backward, looking where it's been instead of where it's going. I would rather tell you about the red-headed woodpeckers who play pretty accordions on Wednesdays high in a weeping willow on the Tombigbee River before breakfast."

They kept on coaxing him, and he told them about the crawfish bird. His face was like a clock telling time, and he made motions with his hands like mittens while telling it, but he didn't move nor shuffle in the least his feet like barges, like tugboats, like canalboats coming home comfortable.

"The crawfish bird," he said, "lives thirty days in the mud and thirty days high in the blue sky. One time far back I talked with a crawfish bird and it talked back to me, telling its explanations and what it could remember just like this: 'Far back I remember I was somewhere, either deep down in the mud or high up in the blue, I can't remember which. And a crawfish and a bird were fighting over whether I should be a crawfish and live with the crawfish or whether I should be a bird and live with the birds. Oh! they were fighting! The crawfish had cut in the air with his claws till the eye of the bird was bleeding. And the bird had ripped the eye of the crawfish till it was bleeding. I cried: "Let me be a bird and a crawfish both"—and it was fixed that way. I love the mud and the crawfishes now, for the mud is nice and warm to sleep in, if you are a crawfish. And the high blue sky up over I love too, for it's grand to fly in if you are a bird among the birds with wings. So here I am with claws and feathers and I asked to have it so.

I shall live and die a crawfish bird. It was fixed that way.' "

Still the girls coaxed him to tell about the Village of Pick Ups. But he wouldn't. And they went away, skipping on their toes and shuffling on their heels and toes, then skipping again.

The old man sat quiet. It was many years ago he had told the story of Pick Ups to the father of Jimmy the Flea. And the father of Jimmy the Flea told it to Jimmy, who told it to Blixie Bimber, his best girl. And she told it to one of the uncles of Wing Tip, who told it to his niece—and she passed it on to Ax Me No Questions. And it was one day in November when the last of the last of the leaves of summer and autumn came off the trees and lay on the ground with a gray November rain falling on them—it was that kind of a day when Ax Me No Questions told the story to her father, Gimme the Ax. It ran like this:

When Pick Ups came here and stayed a few days and talked with the Potato Face Blind Man he had both ears off and he didn't tell anybody but the Potato Face why he had both ears off.

Pick Ups came here from the place where he was born, the Village of Pick Ups, where his home town people lived and where he was raised and grew up. It is a village that used to be, away down in the southeast corner of the Rootabaga Country it used to be. Along the main street and the side streets were hundreds of houses standing hundreds of years. In front of each house was a front door with a front step. And for hundreds of years the people used to open the front doors and sit on the front steps and talk to each other summer evenings. If it was a nice evening, they talked about that. If it looked like rain in the sky, they talked about that. If the baby was getting a new tooth or if the cabbage and the beans were starting to grow pretty and green in the backyards or if the lilacs were coming out with foggy purple blossoms that smelled around the corners of the house, they talked about that. If a boy hit his thumb with a hammer and swore or if a girl came home in a new blue dress with white polka dots, they talked about that.

Then things changed and became different. They found out that if any man took a penny, covered it with whag and then put one drop of slutch on it, the penny had power. Just a copper penny fixed with a little whag and one drop of slutch was stronger than a thousand men. If one penny with a whag cover and a spot of slutch on it was laid on the front doorstep of a house, two minutes afterward the house and the family and everything in the house went straight up overhead, so far in the sky that it was six weeks coming back, six weeks floating down from the sky in fine dust.

This was the same time a long-nose man met a short-nose man one afternoon on the main street. And when they met they bumped against each other not looking, bumping the same as people bump when they bump in an accident.

"You dirty long-nose," said the short-nose man.

"You dirty short-nose," said the long-nose man.

"You long-nose people don't belong," snorted one.

"You short-nose people don't belong," snorted the other.

"Neither do you long-nose people," came back.

Then all the long-nose people and all the short-nose people took pennies and fixed them with whag and slutch. They put these pennies on each other's front doorsteps. And the houses went up in the air overhead, straight into the sky, and took six weeks to come back, floating down in fine dust.

    And so after a while all the long-nose families and all the short-nose families were gone from the Village of Pick Ups. Nobody was left who had either a long nose or a short nose. Only people with middle noses, noses not long and not short, were living in the houses that were left.

    Then one day two men met on the main street with different ears sticking out from their heads. One had ears far out, the other had ears close up. Their ears didn't match.

    And each was proud of his ears. And when they met they bumped against each other not looking, bumping the same as people bump when they bump in an accident.

"You pickled snifter," snorted one.

"You snoof of a snitch," snorted the other.

Then all the people who had ears different from each other began fixing pennies with whag and slutch and sending the houses and families of all those with different ears far and high straight overhead into the sky. So many families with ears sticking out and ears close up went into the air that the young man Pick Ups said to himself, "I am going away to another town and lose my ears. For I have one ear sticking out and the other ear close up and I am liable to be mistaken for belonging in two families. I shall come back with no ears at all and I will be safe."

He was away six weeks. He came back with his ears off. And nobody was there in the Village of Pick Ups to meet him and say hello. All the houses and families were up in the air and falling and floating from the sky in a fine dust coming down thin. Pick Ups felt for his ears and mumbled, "This is a place that used to be and isn't now any more. It feels like there never had been any people or families or houses here." And he wandered around where one time he had seen front doors and front door steps and people sitting out on summer evenings talking to each other about the baby getting its first tooth or the cabbage and beans starting to grow pretty and green in the backyard or lilacs coming out with foggy purple blossoms that smelled around the corner of the house. He nearly cried at one corner where one time he talked with a girl in a new blue dress with white polka dots.

And that is why Pick Ups came here to live with his ears off, never wearing ear muffs in the wintertime. Once he had told the Potato Face Blind Man why his ears were gone. The Potato Face told it to Jimmy the Flea's father. And so it passed on.

When we try to get the Potato Face to tell it as he heard it, he talks to us about little birds that fly upside down on Tuesdays, about the onkatonk that flies backward, looking where it's been instead of where it's going, about the crawfish bird, which is neither a crawfish nor a bird.

The Story of Burnt Chestnuts,
Fish Stars with Fire Tails and Two
Prairie Girls, The Beans Are Burning
and Sweeter Than The Bees Humming

FIVE OR SIX TIMES
A YEAR, SO THEY TELL IT,
THERE ARE FISH STARS COME ON THE SKY
and swim with fire tails in the dark river of the night sky up over the Rootabaga Country.

Now the girl Burnt Chestnuts had her name from the shine of her hair, a dark gold burnish the same as burnt chestnuts. Her father and mother were proud of her and her hair—but not too proud of her and her hair.

In the years she was growing up, the gold burnish of her hair got darker and deeper. She loved to go out on the prairie, alone, and look up at the black river of the night sky when fish stars with fire tails swim out and cross over north and south, east and west. Slow and easy they swim, slow and easy as if they have plenty of time, all the time there is.

Late one evening all the birds sang their sleepy songs whistling and low like and soft like, the same as water running smooth over big red slabs of rock standing alone saying welcome to the water. And these sleepy songs of the birds in the evening made Burnt Chestnuts feel how it is the birds go to sleep high in the sycamores, high in the oaks and cottonwoods, or snuggled alone in hiding places in the tough wire grass. She murmured to herself, "I believe I know how they wink and blink and shut their eyes and stick their heads under their wings and fall with fine thin feathers into sleep."

Long after the sleepy evening songs of the birds, it seemed, Burnt Chestnuts was walking on the prairie alone looking up at the fish stars and the fire tails of the fish stars.

And it seemed to her two shadows were coming across the prairie toward her.
"Shall I run?" she asked herself.
"Shall I pick up my feet and skitter home?"

Then she answered herself, "No, I don't
run—I wait and see what comes—I am a brave
prairie child. I wait."

The two shadows came close. Burnt Chestnuts saw
two girls like herself. One had dark hair like deep midnight
shadows. The other had reddish brown hair like ripe cornsilk
in September. They all said hello to each other pleasant as you
please. Burnt Chestnuts told them she was out on the prairie
the same as every night when the fish stars and fire
tails come on the sky.

"My name is Burnt Chestnuts," she said. "And what
is your name?" looking at the girl with the dark hair.

"The Beans Are Burning."

"What does your mother call you?"

"The Beans Are Burning."

"What does your father call you?"

"The Beans Are Burning."

"What do your brothers and
sisters and next-door playmates,
if you have any, what do they call you?"

"The Beans Are Burning."

"Then it's your really truly name."

"Yes."

"If I write a letter to send you, I must put on the letter it is
for The Beans Are Burning?"

"Yes."

"If your mother calls you for breakfast she says, 'Breakfast is
ready, The Beans Are Burning'?"

"Yes."

"Oh, you are lucky to have such a spoke-special name."

Then Burnt Chestnuts turned to the little girl with the

reddish brown hair standing in the prairie shadows and asked, "What is your name?"

"Sweeter Than The Bees Humming."

"What does your mother call you?"

"Sweeter Than The Bees Humming."

"What does your father call you?"

"Sweeter Than The Bees Humming."

"What do your brothers and sisters and next-door playmates, if you have any, what do they call you?"

"Sweeter Than The Bees Humming."

"If I write a letter to send you, the name I put on the letter must be Sweeter Than The Bees Humming?"

"Yes."

"Oh, you are lucky to have such a spoke-special name."

And now it seemed Burnt Chestnuts asked the two girls why they had come out on the prairie. And they said, first one speaking and then the other, and sometimes both correcting each other or both speaking at once:

"We come out on the prairie to look at the cat stars and the rabbit stars on the sky. One of us—The Beans Are Burning— looks at the long shining cats walking across the sky with

62

shining cats' eyes like wildcats looking out of burnt holes stuck in the sky. One of us—Sweeter Than The Bees Humming— looks at the sky full of rabbits with long fire ears, and by standing still and looking up long she sees the long rabbit ears go longer and go shorter and go longer again."

Then the three girls stood there in the shadows of the prairie and talked about fishes, cats and rabbits on the sky—fish tails of fire, cats' eyes of fire, rabbits' ears of fire, going slow and grand across the sky.

When it was getting late, they all knew they belonged in bed at home. They spoke good-night to each other.

"Good-night, Burnt Chestnuts," said The Beans Are Burning.

"Good-night, The Beans Are Burning," said Burnt Chestnuts.

"Good-night, Burnt Chestnuts," said Sweeter Than The Bees Humming.

"Good-night, Sweeter Than The Bees Humming," said Burnt Chestnuts.

They all started home. Burnt Chestnuts skittered home.

She told her father and mother how she met two shapes on the prairie and when they came up close they were two girls named The Beans Are Burning with hair like deep midnight shadows and Sweeter Than The Bees Humming with reddish brown hair like cornsilk in September. And one saw cat eyes and the other saw rabbit ears of fire in the night sky. And she told them how in the evening before dark in the gloaming she heard the birds sending out sleepy songs soft and whistling and low like running water smooth over big slabs of red rocks saying welcome to the water.

"High in the sycamores, high in the oaks and cottonwoods, and snuggled down in the tough wire grass, they shut their eyes and put their heads under their wings and go to sleep," said Burnt Chestnuts.

Her father had to say, "I think the sleepy songs of the birds put you to sleep and you had a dream on the prairie."

The little girl Burnt Chestnuts walked slow up the stairs, crept into bed and snuggled her head in a big white pillow. "I feel like I have fine thin feathers in my head and fingers," she whispered to herself. Soon she was asleep. Soon the light of the fish stars and fire tails on the sky were shining through the window, falling on a dark gold burnish of hair, on a sleepy dark head in a big white pillow.

How They Are Good
to the Green Hat-Eating Horses

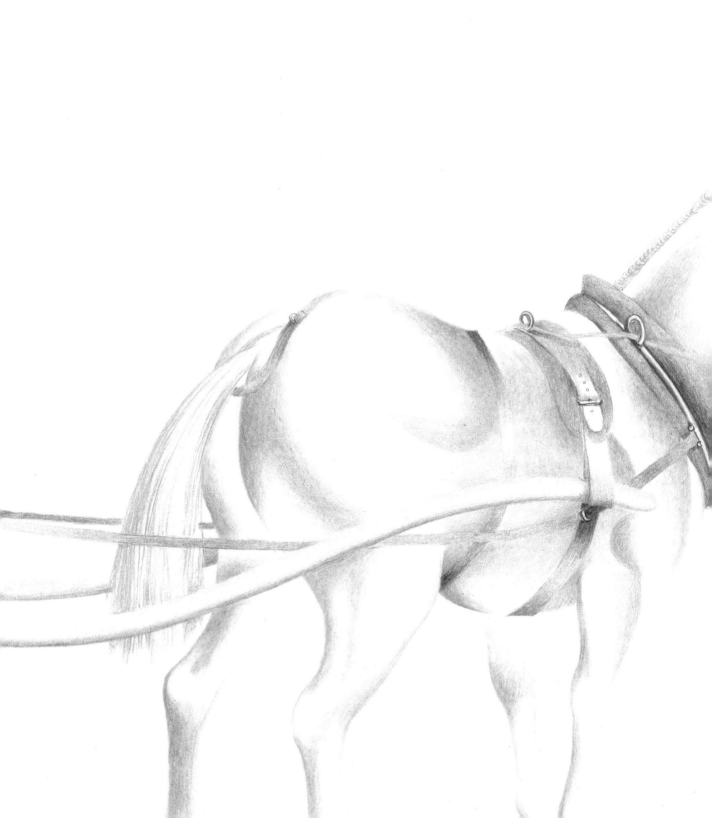

THE FAMOUS
GREEN HAT-EATING

HORSE IS SO CALLED BECAUSE HE IS
green and he eats hats. The people of the Village of Cream
Puffs gave the stranger many explanations why the green
hat-eating horse is green.

"He came from a mountain valley of Greenland's icy mountains," said one citizen. "There is a short green grass grows under snow there and all horses that eat this short grass turn green where the hair grows."

"The green hat-eating horse first became green during one of the long wars between two short wars," said another citizen, who knew the facts because he heard them from his grandfather. "Our cavalry was losing the war. An inventor invented a way to make the horses green. They were so green that they looked like grass. A thousand green horses running on a green valley look like ripe grass in a high wind. It is hard to shoot a green horse running on green grass. So our cavalry won the war. Since then we have always had those green hat-eating horses. We honor them because of their patriotic services to their country. The national flag of our people contains one figure only, the figure of the green hat-eating horse who saved his country in the long war that came between two short wars."

After listening to this explanation the stranger went to a traffic crossing where a traffic policeman was standing and showing the traffic where to go. A green hat-eating horse came along, hitched to a yellow grocery wagon.

"That makes a nice splash," said the stranger to the traffic cop.

"Which does?" asked the cop.

"The green horse and the yellow wagon."

"It's a hot sketch. The law says so. All green horses pull yellow wagons. Wait a little and you'll see all

68

yellow horses pull green wagons. The law says that too."

"Why is the wherefore of this?" asked the stranger.

"Good for the eyes. Green horse and green wagon
too cool. Yellow horse and yellow wagon too hot.
But green horse for yellow wagon and yellow horse
for green wagon, such makes a nice splash."

While they were speaking their spoke, as it happened,
a lady wearing a big round pink picture hat rode by.
Sitting with her was a man with a snoopy silk stovepipe
hat. Behind them was a green hat-eating horse.
One big mouthful and he snapped off the lady's
big round pink picture hat
and chewed it to pieces

and swallowed it one swallow. Another big mouthful and he snapped off the man's snoopy silk stovepipe hat and chewed it to pieces and swallowed it one swallow.

"Why is this?" asked the stranger.

"This is because the green horse is a hat-eating horse and if he didn't eat any hats then nobody would call him hat-eating."

"Who pays for the hats?"

"The hat manufacturers. Look inside any hat here and you see it says the hat manufacturer of that hat guarantees no horses ever will eat the hat but if a green hat-eating horse ever does eat the hat it is guaranteed to be a good hat to eat so it will not make a hat-eating horse sick."

"I see. Then you have very special special hats here."

"Oh yes yes. Corn, oats, bran mash, a little of each is mixed in all our hats so it will be good for the hat-eating horses if they eat your hat or mine."

"I never heard of a city where they are so good to horses like you are good," said the stranger. "You are thoughtful. You give the horses many thoughtfuls, it seems to me."

The Hat Dancers Who Came
the Year Summer Never Came

IT WAS THE YEAR
SUMMER NEVER CAME.
THE BRINGERS OF SUMMER SENT RUNNERS
ahead. "We are coming, summer will soon be here," they
kept on saying, the runners did. And so it went on, the

bringers of summer promising and promising and no summer ever coming until all of a sudden—spiff! Just like that autumn was right among 'em, autumn with her streaks of red and her slashes of purple, autumn was come. And all the promises of the bringers of summer were no use at all because no summer ever came that year. And the people remembered it and talked about it as the year summer never came.

It was a hard year for some people. It was hard for men and women who had promised each other, "Next summer we will get married." Because if you are going to get married in the summer and summer never comes, then you never get married.

It was a hard year for some children. If your father says to you, "Next summer I will surely get you a new wagon, a big wagon with a red painted box and big yellow painted wheels— next summer," and then summer never comes.

Well, that was what happened that year in the Village of Liver-and-Onions. Summer was promised—and lots of other things. Then the spring months dragged out—and spring kept hanging on—and spiff! it was autumn.

Such was the year the hat dancers came to the village. All hat dancers, as you know, are three-legged people and use the third leg to wear their hats on. When they are dancing, also you know, they dance on all three of their legs while they keep all the hats in the air.

The head of the hat dancers who came to the village was a long limber Andalusian who slept on the roof of the hotel. He explained he wasn't particular about it personally, this sleeping on the roof, but the doctor had ordered him posi-tive-ly to sleep where if it should rain he could sit up in bed and watch the rain water run into the eave troughs. He said the doctor believed eave troughs connect with rheumatism and the best way for a dancer to keep away from rheumatism is to sleep on the roof close to the eave troughs.

For breakfast every morning at the hotel the long limber Andalusian who was the head of the hat dancers used to eat a bowl of horseradish. When he was asked why he always had a horseradish breakfast and never anything else to eat the first thing in the morning before starting the day's work, he would answer slow as if he had thought out the answer, "Ask the next horse."

He was always making mysterious answers. The longer the hat dancers stayed and the longer he kept on eating his bowl of horseradish for breakfast and answering people, "Ask the next horse," the more people were saying, "Well, he must have a dark, mysterious past, all right, all right."

The hat dancers stayed in the village weeks and weeks. They gave a performance every night in the Odd Fellows Hall. After a while everybody was talking about the way they danced on three legs while they kept all the hats flying in the air.

The last thing in the show every night, the long limber Andalusian would stand on a big bass drum and drum on the drum with his three legs, keeping the three hats flying in the air around him, and then at last he would throw the hats one by one out over the heads of the audience, out through the front door of the Odd Fellows Hall, out and out—and not one of the hats came back or was ever seen again.

As each hat sailed away out of his hands and out through the door, he would hiss to the hat, "Slip away to the moon, you slicker, and never let us see you come slimpsing back."

The last night they were in the village, the long limber Andalusian delivered a lecture in the high school on the subject "Secrets of the Hat Dancers." He told why three legs were better for dancing than two legs. He explained why he had to eat a bowl of horseradish for breakfast every morning. He explained exactly how every night he threw the hats out over the heads of the audience and out through the door of the Odd Fellows Hall so that the hats never came back and were never found and were all on their way to the moon. Nearly everything puzzling and mysterious was cleared up when he got through lecturing on "Secrets of the Hat Dancers."

At the end of his lecture he said he would answer any questions that the pleasant, courteous citizens of the Village of Liver-and-Onions cared to ask him.

"I got a question," said one man in the audience.

"I will answer you your question—what is it?" said the long limber Andalusian.

"Will you be so good as to tell us how did you get your third leg?"

Then the head of the hat dancers replied without waiting, "It was wished on me."

If you meet people who say this is not a true story tell them the hotel is standing today in the village and anyone who goes there today can see for himself the hotel is standing today and the roof has eave troughs where the hat dancer slept for his rheumatism. In the office of the hotel they will show you the bowl of horseradish from which the three-legged hat dancer ate his bowl of horseradish for breakfast every morning. And exactly across the street is the Odd Fellows Hall and in plain sight is the big front door where the hats came through on their way to the moon in the year summer never came.

The Palace of Pickles and the
Mud Slingers with Buckets of Mud

THE PALACE OF
PICKLES IS A THEATER
DOWNTOWN IN THE VILLAGE OF CREAM

Puffs. It is built of mud. And the walls of it grow thicker
every year because whenever mud slingers in the village

wish to sling mud they go downtown and sling their mud against the walls of the Palace of Pickles.

The chief of police many many years ago called all the policemen into his office and gave them orders. He told them, "Whenever you ketch any mud slingers starting in to sling mud on each other, arrest them and take them down where the Palace of Pickles stands. Make them take along their buckets of mud. Then let half of them stand with their backs to the wall of the Palace of Pickles while the other half of the mud slingers dig their hands down into their buckets and grab handfuls of mud and throw the mud like a firing squad. Then your orders are to let everybody rest an hour. After that it is the turn of the firing squad to stand with their backs to the wall and the rest of the mud slingers will stand with their buckets and throw all they want like a mud slingers firing squad."

Ever since the first chief of police gave this order to the policemen many many years ago, it has been the law of the village.

"Ketch the mud slingers" became the law. And so whenever any boy or young man growing up in the village feels like slinging mud, he knows if he starts and the police see him he will be arrested and taken to the Palace of Pickles, where he is free to sling all the mud he wishes to if he is also willing to stand with his back to the wall and receive on his face all the mud a firing squad of mud slingers wish to throw in his face.

The Palace of Pickles is a theater where they have plays. It is a place where anybody can have a play played. If you write a play and wish to have it played, all you have to do is take it to the Palace of Pickles.

Inside the Palace of Pickles they have two stages, one at one end and the other at the other end of the theater. One stage is a real stage where the actors and actresses walk back and forth and cry and laugh, sing and dance, speak their lines and fade away. The other stage is a looking glass, a big mirror that shows everything going on at the other end of the theater where the real stage is. The audience faces the looking glass. All the chairs in the theater are nailed down and fastened so everybody must look where the looking glass is. This makes it so the backs of the audience are all turned away from where the actors are standing and walking and speaking lines and fading away.

An inventor whose name is forgotten thought up this way to have a theater. It was long ago the inventor thought it up, long ago in the first year when the chief of police said all the mud slingers must come down to the Palace of Pickles to do their mud slinging.

It used to happen that nearly all the audiences in the Palace of Pickles were mud slingers carrying their buckets of mud. If they did not like the play being played they would stand up with hands full of mud and throw the mud into the faces of the actors and actresses on the real stage. The inventor thought if the seats were changed the other way so the audience would be sitting with their backs to the real stage they could see the play just as well if a big looking glass made a second stage. So now when the mud slingers don't like the play, they have lots of fun throwing mud at the actors and actresses on the looking glass. Between the acts gangs of washers come out with sponges and chamois skins and clean off the looking glass and the next act is played and the mud slingers have all the fun they want and it costs nobody nothing.

How the Fairies Went Away...
and Who Took Their Places

SPINK AND
SKABOOTCH, TWO GIRLS,
ONE OLDER THAN THE OTHER, ONE
younger than the other, came one day to the Old Slicker,
a man who lives in the same house with them. It was

summertime and Spink and Skabootch came with questions to ask the Old Slicker. The wind was dancing wind dances over the oat fields and the timothy hay fields. And the sun was shining down on the tops of the oats and the hay, showing a haze gold on the oats and a haze green silver on the hay.

"Tell us about the fairies," said Spink and Skabootch.

"They are all gone away," said the Old Slicker, whittling with a whittling knife. "They came to me and spoke good-by and gave me postage stamps and told me I should write letters to them."

"You make us feel sorry the fairies are all gone away," said Spink and Skabootch. "All day we are going to be sorry and all day tomorrow we are going to be sorry."

"Why don't you ask me something else you ought to be asking me?" asked the Old Slicker.

"You make us so sorry we don't want to ask you anything else because the fairies are gone away," was the answer of Spink and Skabootch.

"Why don't you ask me what I am going to write in the letters I stick the postage stamps on when I write letters to the fairies who are gone away?"

"Oh, oh, oh, tell us, tell us."

Then the Old Slicker loosened up, whittled slower and slower with his whittling knife, took a long thoughtful look at the oat fields and the timothy hay fields and said:

"I shall begin one letter, 'Dear Fairies.' And I shall tell them, 'I am sorry you are gone and Spink and Skabootch are sorry you are gone.'

88

Then I shall tell them thousands and thousands of little fixers have come to take their places. For every one of the old time fairies there is a beautiful little fixer.

"If you go into the oat field and stoop over way down low you will see the wheelbarrow fixers. They are bringing the wheelbarrows full of gold that change the oats from green to gold. Yellow dusty gold dust is all over them. They are yellow shiny gold from the tops of their flat heads to the bottoms of their flat feet.

"Four hands they have, two hands for pushing the wheelbarrow, and two hands for shoveling the gold dust into the wheelbarrow. Shiny, all shiny the insides of their four hands are, shiny from pushing the handles of the wheelbarrow and holding the handles of the gold shovels for shoveling gold dust. In the nighttime when it is dark and there is no moon and even the stars are hiding, when it is pitch dark, if you stoop over and look deep down in the oats, you will see four spots shining close together like a four-spot domino—it is the four hands of one of the oat fixers.

"They have flat feet to stand on each other's heads. And they have flat heads to hold each other's flat feet on. Sometimes six fixers stand one after the other on top of each other, pushing their wheelbarrows with two hands and holding their shovels in the other hands. Six fixers one on top of the other go up high enough sometimes. Other times, when the oat straw is growing higher and higher and the oats fastened to the straw is nearly ripe, then sixty-six fixers have to stand on top of each other, the bottom one with his flat feet on the ground and all the others each one having his flat feet on the flat head of the fixer next under him. It is fun to hear them count to sixty-six, the first man down on the bottom saying, 'One,' the next, 'Two,' and so on up and up, 'Five,' 'Ten,' 'Thirty,' 'Fifty,' till we hear the top fixer, the last one, call 'Sixty-six.'

"Jumping with their flat feet on the tops of each other's heads, the heads are all hard and flat on top. Their feet are so flat and their heads are so flat that sometimes when the wind is blowing hard and all the fixers are feeling reckless they climb one on top of the other till they are six hundred fixers high. Then they count, the bottom fixer, 'One,' the next one 'Two,' and so on till the last fixer, the top one, calls off, 'Six hundred.' It is a game and they call it Six Hundred.

"It is these fixers who change the oats from green in early June to gold in the middle of July. There are thousands of them, all dusty with gold oat dust, running and pushing their wheelbarrows of oat gold dust till all of the oat fields for miles and miles are shining with a haze gold over and a haze gold under and between."

The Old Slicker brushed away some shavings of wood and smiled at Spink and Skabootch.

"If you stoop over and look far down to the black dirt where the roots of the oat stalks are, the most wonderful of all are the ladder lads. They are fixers too, but everybody calls them ladder lads. Each ladder lad carries a ladder, and his ladder means more to him than anything else. He sleeps with his ladder over him and under him like a double blanket. He fries eggs in his ladder. He combs his hair with his ladder. He puts it over his head for an umbrella when rain comes.

"The work of the ladder lads is to climb up on their ladders, up where the oats are fastened onto the oat straws, and there watch and keep watch to be sure the oats stay on where they ought to stay. If one ladder won't reach up they take two ladders put together. If two ladders won't reach up they put three ladders together. If three ladders won't reach they put four ladders together. And so on. And so on. They put enough ladders together to reach up to where they want to go for watching and keeping watch where the oats are fastened to the oat straws. It is these ladder lads who keep the fasteners fastened so the oats never drop off the straws.

"When a rainstorm blows over the oat fields the ladder lads get out and put their ladders together and climb up to watch and keep watch so the oats stay on the straw. And as they climb up on their ladders while the rain comes washing and pouring down they keep their necks and ears dry by holding their ladders over their heads like umbrellas."

Spink and Skabootch broke in. "Make us one, will you?"

"Make you one what?" asked the Old Slicker.

"A ladder like the ladder lads have, a ladder you climb up and stand on while you hold it over your head like an umbrella."

"Yes, I will make you one next Monday and another one next Tuesday," said the Old Slicker before going on again.

"After the rainstorm is over the ladder lads begin the famous ladder dance. It is a wonderful dance but it is hard unless you know how—and only the ladder lads know how. In this ladder dance they are all the time climbing down from their ladders and never climbing up. How they get to the tops of their ladders so they can climb down without climbing up is the queer part of the dance.

"Sometimes it looks as though the ladders jump and dance all by themselves. And if you listen sharp sometimes you can hear the ladder lads telling stories about how the ladders get up all alone in the middle of the night and dance in squares, dance in circles, dance straight up and upside down, turn handsprings and somersaults, and flip-flop each other in crazy flip-flops like the letter Z at the end of the alphabet.

"The dance goes on all night long. The only light they have is the shining of the gold steps and gold sides of the ladders themselves. The dance goes on till daylight begins to open winkers in the sky of the east. Then the ladder dancers all stand with their feet close together singing a soft starlight song to the last of the white stars in the sky just before daylight. Then each of the ladders goes to lay himself down and sleep like a million dollars apiece."

The Old Slicker stopped talking and looked again across the oat fields and the timothy hay fields, whittling with his whittling knife. A pile of splinters and shavings up to his ankles lay at his feet.

"I have whittled too much today and I have talked too much today," he said, running his right hand through the hair of Spink soft as thistledown, and his left hand through the hair of Skabootch soft as thistledown.

And Spink put her head half-sleepy on the Old Slicker's left knee while Skabootch put her head half-sleepy on the Old Slicker's right knee.

And each of them said, the two of them speaking together the same thought, "I'm not sorry at all now, sorry no more at all now."

It was then the Old Slicker put away his whittling knife and stopped whittling and said again, "I have whittled too much today and I have talked too much today."

CARL SANDBURG is fondly remembered as America's unofficial poet laureate. He was also a biographer and historian. His monumental six-volume biography of Abraham Lincoln won the Pulitzer Prize for history in 1940, and in 1951 his *Complete Poems* won the Pulitzer Prize for poetry. A champion of the common man, Sandburg had an absorbing interest in American ballads, folk tales, and legends, which is reflected in his work. He died in 1967.

PAUL O. ZELINSKY is a well-known illustrator of children's books, including the Caldecott Honor books *Rumpelstiltskin* and *Hansel and Gretel*. He is also the illustrator of *The Wheels on the Bus* and *The Random House Book of Humor for Children*. Born in Evanston, Illinois, Mr. Zelinsky graduated from Yale University and Tyler School of Art, and now lives in New York City with his wife and daughters.

GEORGE HENDRICK is Professor of English at the University of Illinois at Urbana-Champaign. A Sandburg scholar, he edited the second volume of Sandburg's autobiography, *Ever the Winds of Chance*, with Margaret Sandburg, and *Fables, Foibles, and Foobles*, a collection of Sandburg humor.